Early Sunday Morning

Early Sunday Morning

DENENE MILLNER

ILLUSTRATED BY VANESSA BRANTLEY-NEWTON

A DENENE MILLNER BOOK

BOLDEN

AN AGATE IMPRINT

CHICAGO

Printed in China

Early Sunday Morning
ISBN 13: 978-1-57284-211-3
ISBN 10: 1-57284-211-3
ebook ISBN 13: 978-1-57284-794-1
ebook ISBN 10: 1-57284-794-8
First printing: April 2017

10 9 8 7 6 5 4 3 2 1   17 18 19 20 21

Bolden is an imprint of Agate Publishing. Agate books
are available in bulk at discount prices. Learn more at
agatepublishing.com.

For my mother, Bettye, who taught me how to love God,
and my father, Jimy, who taught me how to love myself.
That's love. —DM

For Mama Shirley, who taught us to sing, pray, and praise,
and to rise early Sunday mornings. —VBN

Sunday is the Lord's day, when Mommy, Daddy, my brother, and I go to church. This Sunday is extra special because I'll be singing my first solo in the youth choir.

I sing lots of songs in the mirror when no one is watching. Sometimes, Daddy and I sing loud, silly songs together and giggle at the funny words. Singing with Daddy is when I am happiest of all.

But singing by myself with a microphone in front of a crowd is big. And a little scary. Even at choir rehearsal when barely anyone is watching me practice, my voice gets all trembly.

One day, I heard Angela and Tommy whisper and giggle as I walked back to my seat. "Good grief, Sister Sarah could have just given that solo to a goat. It might not remember the words, but at least it would be able to sing the notes." Their words stung. So did my tears.

Everybody knows I am nervous, and so they all tell me their ideas for how I can sing my song strong and clear. Auntie thinks wearing a new dress will help. "Looking fancy makes you feel brave!" she promises.

Even Mr. Harvey, the barber, adds in his two cents. "See, what you have to do is pretend everyone in the audience has a big ol' watermelon head. You'll be too busy laughing to be scared," he says as he spins my brother, Troy, around in the chair.

The night before my big solo, Mommy washes
my hair with strawberry shampoo and sits me on
pillows while she twists it into a beautiful crown.

Sometimes, if I sit really still and don't make too
much of a fuss, she lets me have a bowl of ice
cream. But I am fidgety. "Tomorrow you'll sing your
song so pretty, the angels will shout in Heaven,"
she says. "Believe that with all your heart."

"I will," I say quietly.

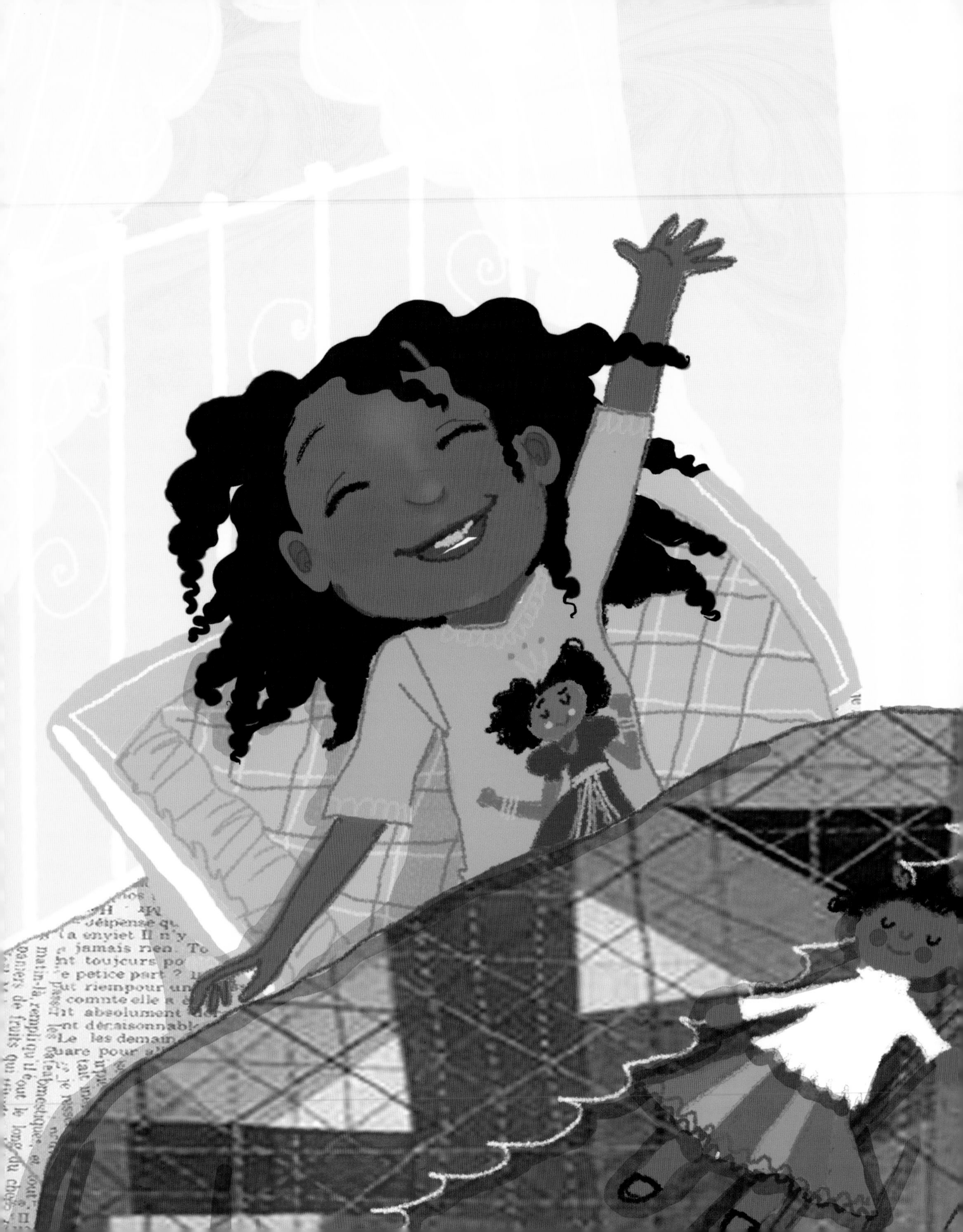

Early Sunday morning is when the magic happens. A gentle nudge and it's rise and shine, give God the glory!

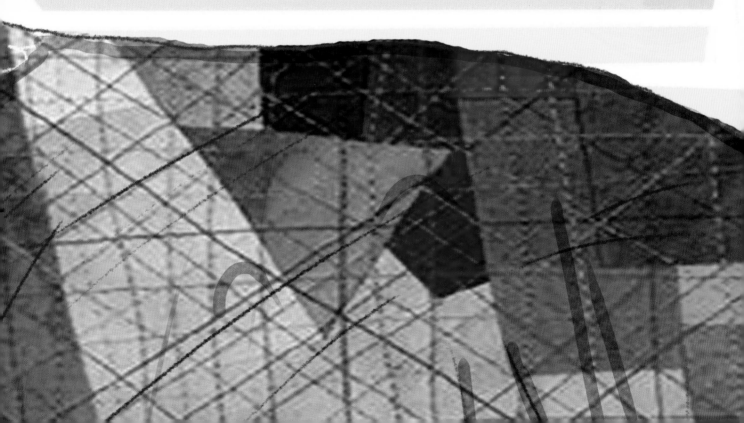

Troy and I wake up to the smell of roast beef, macaroni and cheese, collards, corn bread, and sweet potato pie—my favorite. Mommy always makes Sunday dinner in the morning so we can eat right after church. That's because sometimes, when Pastor Scott gets lost in the rhythm, he can preach on . . . and on . . . and on . . . waaaaay into the afternoon. We eat cereal and toast to hold us over until dinnertime.

After breakfast, I brush my teeth and wash my face and check my hair while Mommy lays out my church clothes: New dress. Tights. And my Mary Janes, shined up like a new penny.

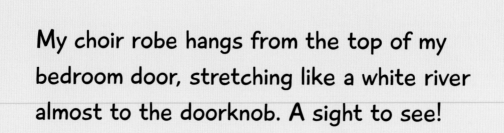

My choir robe hangs from the top of my
bedroom door, stretching like a white river
almost to the doorknob. A sight to see!

Troy steps out of his room cool as you please in his suit and tie, looking just like Daddy when he takes Mommy out dancing. He giggles when he sees me twirling in my fancy dress.

We both watch Mommy swoosh gloss across her lips. When she gives a little tug at her church hat and pinches each of our cheeks, Troy and I know it's almost time to go.

We wake Daddy to hug and kiss him goodbye. He worked an extra shift at the bakery, so on this Sunday, he will have to rest. Daddy won't be coming to see me sing. This makes me sad.

But he gives me peppermints and money for the offering, plus a hug and lots of kisses to help me be brave. "If you get nervous, just pick a spot in the church and sing to it like you do your mirror," he says. "Daddy will be there with you in spirit, singing along with you." Knowing this will have to do.

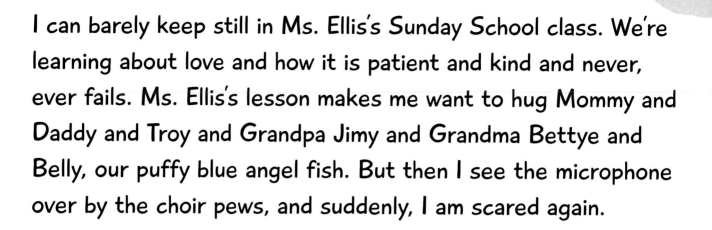

I can barely keep still in Ms. Ellis's Sunday School class. We're learning about love and how it is patient and kind and never, ever fails. Ms. Ellis's lesson makes me want to hug Mommy and Daddy and Troy and Grandpa Jimy and Grandma Bettye and Belly, our puffy blue angel fish. But then I see the microphone over by the choir pews, and suddenly, I am scared again.

I watch the hands on the clock as the collection plate is passed . . . and Deacon Claytor reads the announcements . . . and little Kelvin makes the whole Sunday School laugh when he prays for God to make Pastor Scott's sermon end early enough for him to watch the football game.

After Sunday School, Mommy helps me into my robe. Then she folds my hands into hers and gives me that knowing look—one that says, "Everything is going to be all right." I want to believe that. At least, I try.

When our youth choir marches through the doors, every eye is on us. We float down the aisle like an army of angels, lifting our voices in praise all the way up to the rafters. And right there in the front pew is Mommy, smiling and singing and shaking her tambourine.

I fidget while Pastor Scott welcomes the visitors and leads the prayer. Then the notes to my song rise up from the organ. Ms. Jackson's fingernails tap loudly against the keys as the melody fills the church. "Praise him!" I hear my mother say. "Tell it to the Lord," one of the deaconesses shouts.

I don't look at the choir director or even my mother. I do not imagine watermelons or remember what my dress looks like. Instead, I pick a spot to focus on, just like Daddy told me to, and I lean into the microphone as I stare at the double doors.

And just when I swallow really hard . . .
And take a deep breath . . .
And get ready to sing my first note . . .
The double doors swing open . . .

And there is Daddy, standing tall and
handsome with a smile outshined only by
mine! "Sing, baby," he shouts.

I lift my voice and sing with the might of the angels—just like I do when I'm alone in my room dancing in front of my mirror, and when Daddy is singing alongside me, too.

And the church shouts, "Amen!"

ABOUT DENENE MILLNER BOOKS

Denene Millner Books are published under the direction of *New York Times* bestselling author, editor, and parenting authority Denene Millner, as part of Agate's Bolden imprint, which is devoted to the work of African American writers. Its offerings focus on diverse stories for young readers that celebrate the everyday wonders of life among African American youth and families.